Prancing, Dancing LILY

by Marsha Diane Arnold

pictures by John Manders

Dial Books for Young Readers  New York

For my father, his Ayrshire dream, and all the cows at Highland Ayr dairy farm—M.D.A.

For Mom—J.M.

Published by Dial Books for Young Readers. A division of Penguin Young Readers Group. 345 Hudson Street, New York, New York 10014. Text copyright © 2004 by Marsha Diane Arnold. Pictures copyright © 2004 by John Manders. All rights reserved. Designed by Lily Malcom. Text set in Cochin. Manfactured in China on acid-free paper. Library of Congress Cataloging-in-Publication Data. Arnold, Marsha Diane. Prancing, dancing Lily / by Marsha Diane Arnold ; pictures by John Manders.   p. cm.   Summary: Lily will someday be the "Bell Cow," leading her herd, but because her prancing and dancing only disrupts their order, she travels the world looking for the right place and dance for her. ISBN 0-8037-2823-9 [1. Cows—Fiction. 2. Dance—Fiction. 3. Self-realization—Fiction.] I. Manders, John, ill. II. Title. PZ7.A7363 Pr 2004   [Fic]—dc21   2002005852

10 9 8 7 6 5 4 3 2 1

Notes on technique: John begins an illustration with a pencil sketch on layout bond paper. He then traces the sketch onto watercolor paper and paints the shadow and color using watercolors. The highlights and accents are added with gouache and color pencil to redraw the sketch on top of the colors. This way, the fun of the sketch is preserved in the final illustration.

"Come on in, Rose! Milking time!" Farmer Gibson called across the pasture.

Clang-a-lang. Clang-a-lang. All the cows fell in behind Rose. Except for Lily. Prancing, dancing Lily.

"Stop zigzagging through the line, Lily," said Violet. "You're making us dizzy."

"Ow!" yelled Daisy. "Watch those high-kicking hooves!"

Lily skipped to the pond and twirled around the willow tree.

"That Lily is all over the pasture," said Marigold. "When she's Bell Cow, it will take us all night to get to the barn."

"She'll never be able to lead the line," said Violet. "She can't even stay in line."

Lily pretended not to hear, but she couldn't help thinking that they were right. Lily's Grandmoo Iris had led the most orderly cow lines in Wisconsin. And Lily's Mamoo Rose always won "Best Bell Cow" at the state fair. Soon it would be Lily's turn to lead the herd. But whenever she was around, there was confusion on the cow trail.

"Somewhere in the world, there must be a place for a dancing Bell Cow," said Lily as she stared beyond the fence posts.

Just then, a gust of wind blew a magazine into the pasture.

On every page, there was prancing and dancing! Quickly, Lily made her decision.

She left a note for Mamoo on the willow tree.

Lily pranced and danced down Farmer Gibson's driveway, then onto County Road 14. Across the valley, she heard tail-whisking music spilling out of a big red barn.

As the fiddles zinged and the caller called, Lily joined the sashay. But she circled right when she should have circled left.

Recovering on a bale of hay, Lily borrowed some paper and a pen.

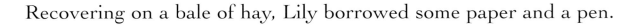

My dear Mamoo
(and the herd too),

I do-si-doed, I spun the top,
And then I did the belly flop!
This square dancing
is quite a whirl,
But maybe I'm a city girl.

Lily

Lily traveled the back roads until she reached New York City. Prancing and dancing past Rockefeller Center, she saw an audition sign outside Radio City Music Hall.

"We have a camel and hundreds of Santas, but we've never had a dancing cow. How spectacular!" said the director.

But on opening night, Lily kicked her hooves so high,
they got tangled in the Christmas tree lights.

She exited early, twinkling all the way to the Empire State Building.
At the Big Apple Café, she sent a postcard home.

My dear Mamoo
   (and the herd too),
I kicked my hooves with so much flair,
The lights and tree fell everywhere.
Instead of cheers, I heard loud boos.
I think I need an ocean cruise.
                              Lily

Mamoo Rose
c/o Farmer Gibson
One Dairy Road
Ayrshire, WI
      54991

Lily boarded the *Holiday Happiness* cruise ship the very next day. Talia, the lead tap dancer, invited Lily to join the dance troupe. "Your hooves make perfect little tap shoes," she said.

But at the captain's dinner that night, Lily tip-tap-tripped right into the chocolate mousse.

After a hot bath, Lily wrote a letter on the ship's stationery.

When the *Holiday Happiness* reached shore, everyone wished Lily well. "Keep searching, Lily," said Talia. "I'm sure you'll find a place just right for you.

Around the world, Lily danced.
She stamped a feisty flamenco in Spain,
swayed on stilts in Senegal,

flew at the ballet in Russia,
and swung her hips to the belly dance in Turkey.

Finally, Lily arrived on a small island in the Caribbean. She looked across the waters and thought of Farmer Gibson's pond.

Then she faxed a message home.

My dear Mamoo (and the herd too),

My hooves have never been so sore.
Can't find the place I'm looking for.
I miss the herd. I miss the bell.
Some days I'm sad I said farewell.

Lily

As Lily sat with her head in her hooves, she heard drumming in the distance.

Boom-boom-boom-boom-boom. Boom.

Boom-boom-boom-boom-boom. Boom.

Winding through the street was the longest line she had ever seen.
"Come join our conga!" someone shouted to Lily.
Lily took her place behind the last person in line. Then someone danced up behind her.

Everyone pranced and danced. They zigzagged this way and that way, following the lead of the drummer. But it was always a perfect line.

"Back home we lead lines with a bell," Lily told her new friend, Ricardo.

"There are lots of ways to lead a line. We like a conga drum."

They ended up at Ricardo's home, where everyone was invited to stay for dinner.

Lily borrowed Ricardo's computer to write an exuberant e-mail home.

TO: MamooRose@farmtrails.com

My dear Mamoo (and the herd too),

Guess what! I know the place for me.
And a dance that fits us perfectly.
We'll dance a line with drum and bell.
I'm coming home now. All is well.

Lily

One bright morning, Lily came home drumming.

Boom-boom-boom-boom-boom. Boom.

Boom-boom-boom-boom-boom. Boom.

Mamoo Rose and the whole herd trotted out to greet her.

All day, Lily showed them how to prance and dance in a conga line. Everyone took turns being the drummer.

"Finally, Lily has a good idea," said Violet, drumming around the willow tree.

"We'll be the only drumming Bell Cows in Wisconsin," said Daisy.

"We'll be famous all the way to Minnesota," said Marigold.

"Come on in, Rose. Milking time!" Farmer Gibson called across the pasture.

Mamoo Rose turned to Lily. "I think Farmer Gibson is calling you," she said, placing her bell around Lily's neck.

All the cows fell in behind Lily.

Boom-boom-boom-boom-boom. Clang-a-lang.
Boom-boom-boom-boom-boom. Clang-a-lang.

And together they pranced and danced back to the barn.

To my friends (both near and far),
You all were kind to take a chance
And let me join your special dance.
I wish that you could see me now,
The prancing, dancing conga cow.

            Lily

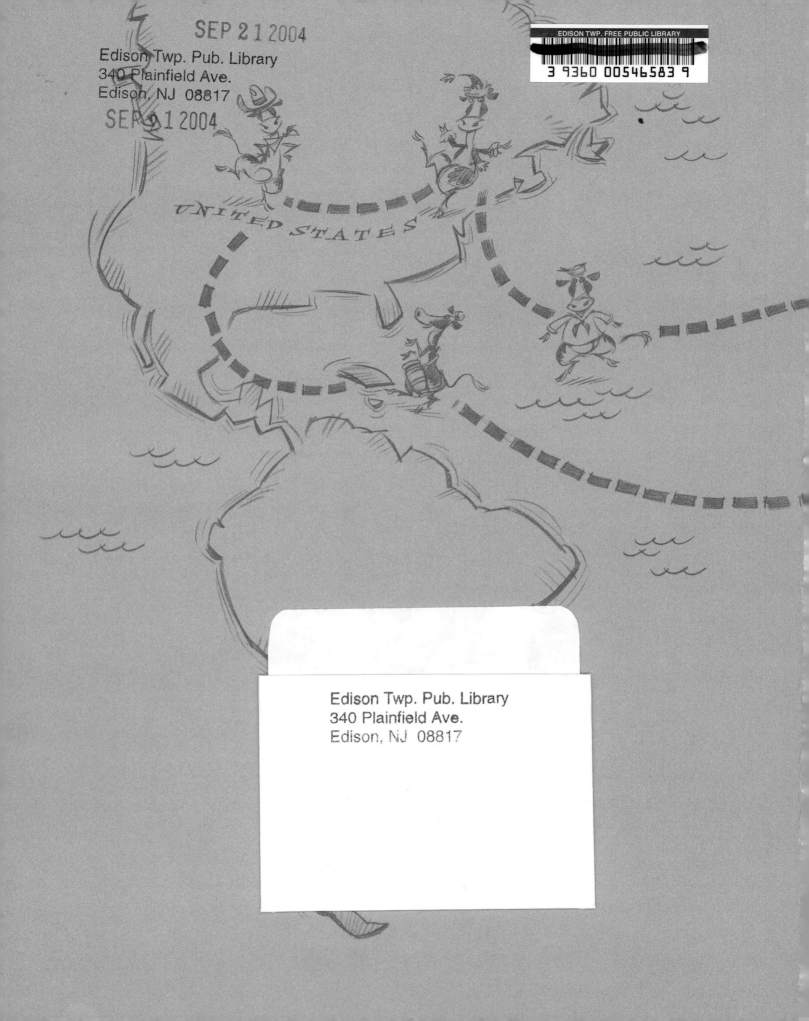